When a truck is "in transit,"
it is on the move.

A cement mixer has two jobs.
One job is to mix the cement.

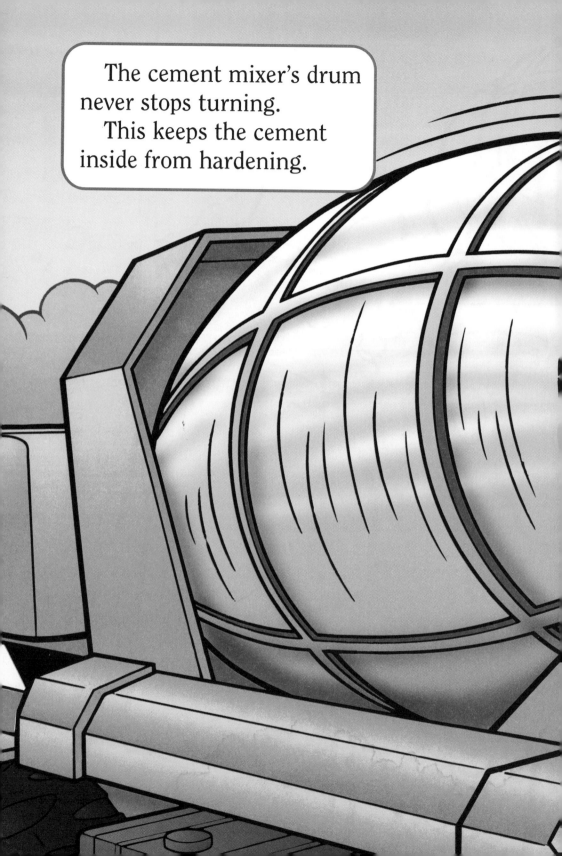

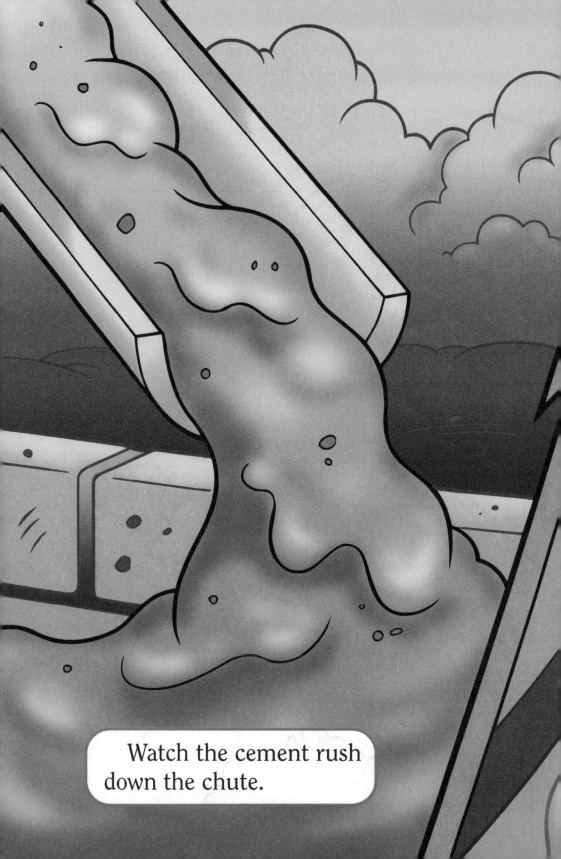

Watch the cement rush
down the chute.

It's just like going down a slide into a swimming pool. Look out below!

Concrete hardens when it dries. Uh-oh. Be careful where you step!

Now take a look inside the truck.
The driver sits in the cab.

The cab has a steering wheel, gas pedal, and brake—just like your car.